Abe Lincoln Remembers

When I was little,
the cabin we lived in was small
with one room and one window.
At first I thought the sky was square
like a piece of cut cloth.
I could only see two birds in the sky
and one squirrel in the tree.

ANN TURNER

Abe Lincoln Remembers

PICTURES BY WENDELL MINOR

HarperCollinsPublishers

When I got bigger,
Pa told me my legs were like a colt's,
and he was afraid I'd fall down,
they were so long and shanky.
Sometimes I went to school, but
I don't suppose those days would add up
to much more than a year.
I'd fold up my legs like an umbrella
and sit quiet at the back of the schoolroom,
gulping down learning like water.
But Pa wouldn't allow me much schooling,
making me chop wood, build fences,
plant corn, and drive the horses.

I did learn to read, though,
got some history and my numbers.
I'd practice them on the back
of the fire shovel,
for soot and ashes make a fine slate.
And I would do anything for a book.
I'd read any chance I got
and dreamed of freedom,
of rising like a hawk into the sky
to some fine, high place.

*I*t was time to move on.
I left, no money in hand,
no second shirt, just a handkerchief
around a piece of corn bread.
I worked on a flatboat,
and in a general store.

When the storekeeper saw
how I towered over the others,
he bet I'd whip the best
wrestler around—Jack Armstrong.
We locked arms and bodies,
swung back and forth,
then he downed me with a leg throw
the rules did not allow.
But I shook hands with him,
and we became friends.

I knew that being tall is not enough
to make your way in this world.
I needed words for that.
When I studied to become a lawyer,
I practiced my cases out loud as I walked,
learning how to use words
like a leading rein on a colt
to take people where I wanted.
But when I ran for the legislature,
I saw it would take a deal of tugging
to persuade people that slavery was wrong.

*T*hen I found Mary, who agreed
to be my wife.
She was bright and brave
like a flag cracking in the wind,
all color, rustle, and shine.
When I ran for the Senate, she told me,
"You will win, and someday
you will be President."
How I laughed at that!
But later, others thought the same,
and I was nominated to run for the highest office.
I talked and debated
to show people we must be one nation,
not part slave, not part free.

When I won the Presidency,
we took our three sons,
Tad, Willie, and Robert,
to the White House.
They were like balls bounding
down a road, and people said they
had no manners or discipline.
I thought happiness
more important than manners,
though I didn't like it
when Tad drove his cart
and goats down
the White House hall.

But we had need of happiness then:
for the great wound opened in the country
and in my chest—the war.
I tried to keep North and South together,
until it was clear that talk
could not mend this great division.
The dying grieved me so
that I had a joke book in my desk
to keep from weeping.

And I was terrified we would lose.
I could not find good generals,
and we lost as many battles as we won.
But when we won the Battle of Gettysburg,
it seemed the Union might prevail.

*W*hen I went and saw all those graves,
lined up like the rails I used to split,
I could hardly speak.
Words could not lead me here,
and I thought my speech a short, poor thing.
I felt in the middle of some vast tug-of-war,
until I thought my heart would break.

*F*inally our side has won, the country is not divided,
and the slaves are free.
I can be glad of that,
though when I look in the mirror,
I see how sorrow has dug lines in my cheeks.

I told Mary that tonight is a time to be happy.

As we wait to go see a play,

I think again of that little house,

the small window, the piece of sky

with two birds and one squirrel.

How much has come to pass since then.

How much there is still to be done.

A Historical Note

Shy. A dreamer. Strong. Ambitious. So tall he towered over everyone else. One of our greatest Presidents. All these descriptions applied to Abraham Lincoln.

His early years are familiar to us: born into poverty in Kentucky to a stern father and a gentle mother who died when he was still young. Some of the people who knew him then described him as "lazy," as he preferred a book to working in the field.

Leaving home at the age of twenty-two, Lincoln did many things before he settled on becoming a lawyer and going into politics. He worked in a store and as a postmaster, helped a surveyor, and ran for the state legislature in Illinois. There he announced his opposition to slavery.